P9-DCY-303

by maya & matthew

They! they! They! they!

Out on the dance floor we love to
sing they.
They is a way to let everyone
be.
No one left out and everyone
free.
Then when we're friends, we sing
they, she, he, ze.
Making it easy as a-b-c-d.

New friends are everywhere waiting to play!
Let's Dance!

Ari loves to arabesque.
They hold their pose with ease.

Brody is a break dancer.
Brody loves to freeze.

Cory leaps high like a cat.
She springs and leaps and bounds.

Diego drums and dances.
Tree has all the sounds.

Ebony flies everywhere.
They spread their arms like wings.

Fawn is free as a flower.
Fawn can bring the spring.

Gia's going fast and strong.
She's dancing on the go.

Harvey's heart beats happily.
Hip hop makes her flow.

I

Indigo's into insects.
Ze loves the buzzing vibe.

Jorge jams to jazzy tunes.
He or they can jive.

Kelly can kick super high.
His heart lives in the sky.

Lourdes sings of lofty heights.
Their songs let them fly.

m

Marley is a star mermaid.
He or she flows with the sea.

Nathan is a nesting bird.
He just wants to be.

Ocean's arms are open wide.
Tree swings and sways about.

Paul pretends to be a plant.
Paul grows up and OUT.

Quetzal is so, so quiet.
He rests just like a queen.

Rene is into rainbows.
He creates the scene.

Sky is like a star so bright.
All the pronouns are right.

Tai is tiger in the night.
He claims his own might.

Una is a unicorn.
They prance to their own sound.

Viola's a volcano.
Her power's in her ground.

W

Wren whistles when she dances.
She knows just what to do.

Xander exaggerates moves.
They're extremely cool.

Yoli yells YES! joyously.
Their voice becomes the song.

Zahara zooms in and out.
Ze knows that ze belongs.

Now's your chance.
We need your moves.

Join the dance.

There's always room.

Ari
Brody
Cory
Diego
Indigo
Jorge
Kelly
Lourdes
Quetzal
Rene
Sky
Tai
Xander
Yoli
Zahara

Maya makes the art and words. She sings the song to life. Matthew dreams and tinkers. He makes the work tight.

Together they make books for the kids they used to be. And for their own two kids so all kids can grow free!

easy as A, B, C

"...we love to sing they." One way we can make more room to include everybody is by learning the power of *They*! *They* is a great word. It can mean many people or just one and has been used for hundreds of years. When we don't know someone we can begin with *they*. This way we're not making guesses about who they are. We are leaving room for them to be themself. For example, *"Look at that kid dancing. They are amazing!"* If you meet that amazing dancer, they'll probably tell you their name and you'll learn from them which pronoun or pronouns they use to best express the spirit of who they are.

simple as X, Y, Ze

"...we sing they, she, he, ze." There are and have always been more than just **he** and **she**. Throughout time people have played with words to create more room for themselves and their experience. **Ze** is a great example. People have been using **ze** since the 1970s. There are many more, **xe**, **ne**, **ve**, **per**, **thon**... This reminds us that language is changing all the time. Practicing how to use more pronouns than **he** and **she** is a way to free ourselves and each other and stay in the flow.

playful as Tree, Free, Me

Some kids like to use more than one pronoun and may switch back and forth. Some kids don't like any and use their **name**. Some kids create new words. Playing is a valuable way to keep ourselves free. The freer we are the more we are able to grow into our most unique self! For example, **tree** is a playful pronoun to show our connection to nature. If you want to play more with **tree** check out Maya's other book, *Call Me Tree*. Know that you are free to be who you fully are and to claim the words or make new ones that show your unique self to others!

Being inclusive is as easy as A-B-C

For Educational Tools, Games and More visit us online!

PLAYINGWITHPRONOUNS.COM
GENDERWHEEL.COM

more from M+M

They She He Me: Free to Be!

Want to explore even more about pronouns? Check out the companion book and you'll see some familiar faces.

Playing with Pronouns game cards

Play with all the kids from the pronoun books! Simple sorting and matching games to break down stereotypes and assumptions.

The Gender Wheel: a story about bodies and gender for every body

Written & illustrated by Maya & geared toward ages 7-10. Explores gender in relation to colonization and how to move beyond the binary into holistic, nature-based ways of thinking using the Gender Wheel, a tool to express the dynamic, infinite and inclusive reality of gender.

For Sky & Zai, may you always be free! -M+M

with consultation from Matthew SG
Published by Reflection Press, San Francisco, CA

ISBN 978-1-945289-17-0 (hardcover)
ISBN 978-1-945289-18-7 (paperback)
Library of Congress Control Number: 2019903191
Book Design & Production by Matthew SG

Summary: Inclusive pronouns are learned alongside the alphabet in this joyously illustrated take on the classic ABC book.

The Gender Wheel® books support The Gender Wheel Curriculum, a holistic, nature-based approach to understanding gender. Inclusive perspectives and practices at every level of the curriculum support a strong sense of self, while creating systemic change in the world at large.

Reflection Press is a POC queer and trans owned independent publisher of radical and revolutionary children's books and works that expand cultural and spiritual awareness. Rooted in holistic, nature-based and anti-oppression frameworks, our materials support a strong sense of individuality along with a community model of real inclusion. Visit us at **www.reflectionpress.com**

For permissions, bulk orders, or if you receive defective or misprinted books, please contact us at info@reflectionpress.com

CPSIA information can be obtained
at www.ICGtesting.com
Printed in the USA
LVHW070148210122
709008LV00002B/2